Those green things

Those green things

by
Kathy Stinson

illustrated by
Deirdre Betteridge

Annick Press
Toronto • New York

Annick Press gratefully acknowledges the support
of the Canada Council and the Ontario Arts Council.

Canadian Cataloguing in Publication Data
Stinson, Kathy
    Those green things

ISBN 1-55037-377-3 (bound) ISBN 1-55037-376-5 (pbk.)

I. Betteridge, Deirdre. II. Title.

PS8587.T56T46 1994   jC813'.54 C94-931737-3
PZ7.S75Th 1994

The art in this book was rendered in watercolours.
The text was typeset in Garamond by Attic Typesetting.

Distributed in Canada by:
Firefly Books Ltd.
250 Sparks Avenue
Willowdale, ON
M2H 2S4

Published in the U.S.A. by Annick Press (U.S.) Ltd.
Distributed in the U.S.A. by:
Firefly Books (U.S.) Inc.
P.O. Box 1338
Ellicott Station
Buffalo, NY 14205

Printed and bound in Canada by
Metropole Litho Inc.

Dedicated with thanks to Katie for her
curiosity about my lunch.
K.S.

For Adam and Emily
with love.
D.B.

W

hat are those green
things?
What green things?
Those green things in the
laundry basket.

*Those green things in the
laundry basket are your
socks.*
Oh, I thought they were…

…lizards eating my
T-shirts.

W hat are those green
things?
What green things?
Those green things in my
scrambled egg.

*Those green things in your
scrambled egg are spinach.
It's an omelette.*
Oh, I thought they were…

...bugs and worms that
weren't ripe yet.

What are those green
things?
What green things?
Those green things in the
closet.

Those green things in the closet are bags full of old clothes.
Oh, I thought they were…

...lumpy bumpy monsters
hiding till I came to find my
boots.

W hat are those green
things?
What green things?
Those green things on the
windowsill.

Those green things on the windowsill are crayons. You left them there and they melted in the sun.

Oh, I thought they were…

...the green beans
Gregory wouldn't eat at
dinner yesterday.

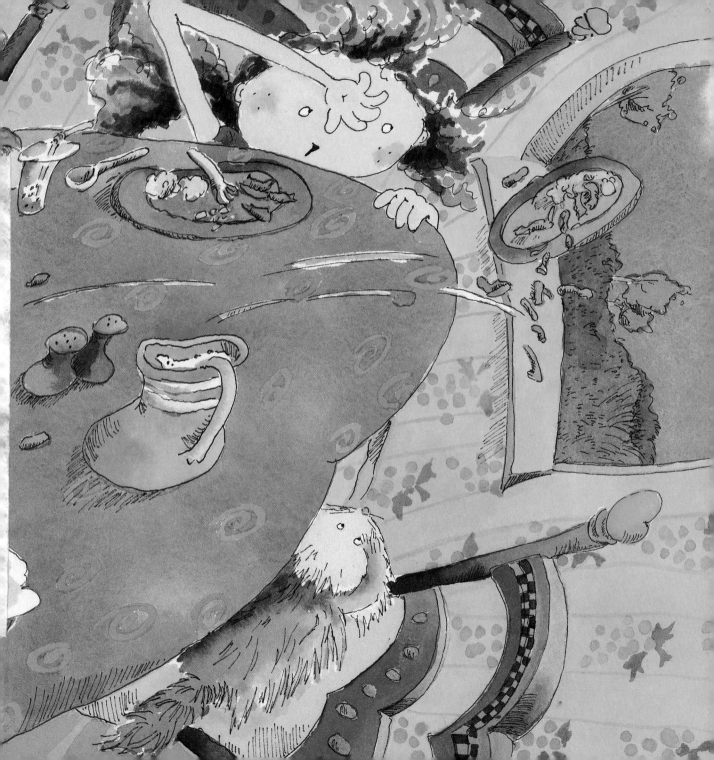

What are those green things?
What green things?
Those green things in the garage.

Those green things in the garage are garden hoses.
Oh, I thought they were…

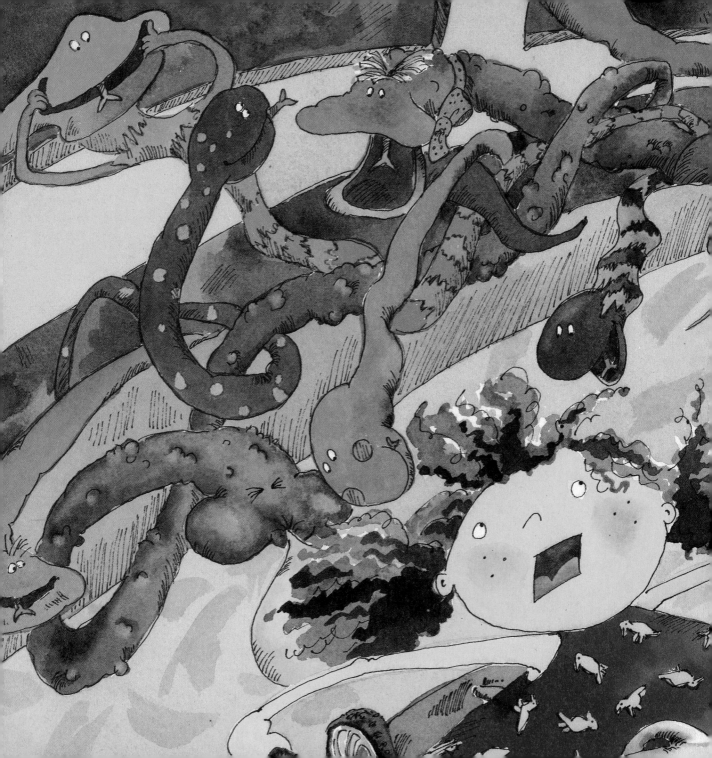

...slithery snakes sneaking
through the window.

What are those green
things?
What green things?
Those green things on the
porch.

Those green things on the porch are Martians. They are coming to take me to Mars so you can't ask me any more questions about those green things. **What green things?**

*Those green things in the
laundry basket.
Those green things in your
scrambled egg.
Those green things in the
closet.
Those green things on the
windowsill.
Those green things in the
garage.
Those green things on the
porch.*

Mom?
Yes?

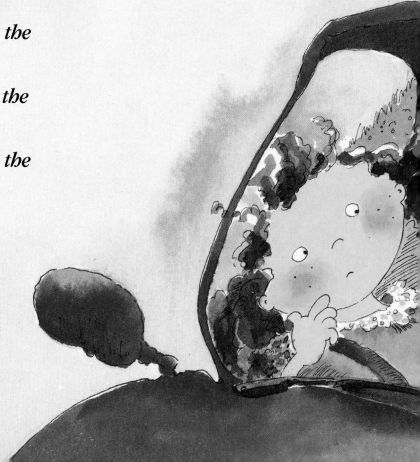

What are those green
things in your sandwich?

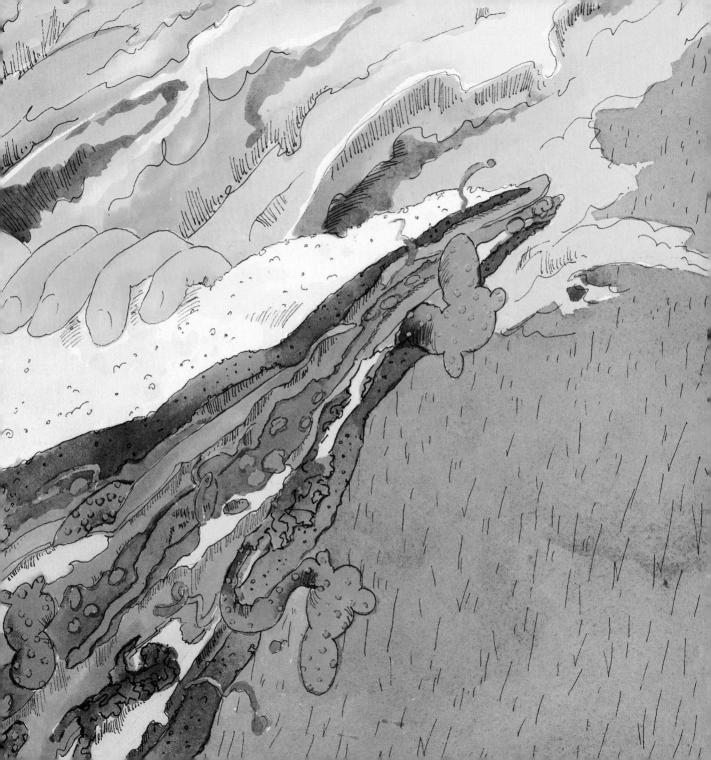

**Other Picture Books by Kathy Stinson,
published by Annick Press**

Red is Best

Big or Little?

The Bare Naked Book

The Dressed Up Book

Mom and Dad Don't Live Together Any More